SPIDERS SET I

BIRD-EATING SPIDERS

Tamara L. Britton
ABDO Publishing Company

visit us at
www.abdopublishing.com

Published by ABDO Publishing Company, 8000 West 78th Street, Edina, Minnesota 55439. Copyright © 2011 by Abdo Consulting Group, Inc. International copyrights reserved in all countries. No part of this book may be reproduced in any form without written permission from the publisher. The Checkerboard Library™ is a trademark and logo of ABDO Publishing Company.

Printed in the United States of America, North Mankato, Minnesota.
042010
092010

 PRINTED ON RECYCLED PAPER

Cover Photo: iStockphoto
Interior Photos: AP Images p. 7; iStockphoto pp. 5, 9, 11, 12, 15, 21;
   Peter Arnold pp. 17, 19, 20

Editor: Megan M. Gunderson
Art Direction & Cover Design: Neil Klinepier

Library of Congress Cataloging-in-Publication Data

Britton, Tamara L., 1963-
  Bird-eating spiders / Tamara L. Britton.
     p. cm. -- (Spiders)
  Includes bibliographical references and index.
  ISBN 978-1-61613-439-6
  1. Theraphosa blondi--Juvenile literature. I. Title.
  QL458.42.T5B745 2011
  595.4'4--dc22
                                          2010009625

CONTENTS

BIRD-EATING SPIDERS 4
SIZES 6
SHAPES 8
COLORS 10
WHERE THEY LIVE 12
SENSES 14
DEFENSE 16
FOOD 18
BABIES 20
GLOSSARY 22
WEB SITES 23
INDEX 24

BIRD-EATING SPIDERS

    Spiders are arachnids. Scorpions, ticks, and mites are arachnids, too. Arachnids have two body parts and eight legs. Spiders are also arthropods. So, their skeletons are on the outside of their bodies. And, spiders are ectothermic. Ectotherms get their body heat from their surroundings.

    Scientists recognize 109 spider families. Within these families there are 38,000 species! About 800 species belong to the family **Theraphosidae**.

    Very large members of this family are known by different names in different parts of the world. In North America, these huge spiders are called tarantulas. They are called baboon spiders in Africa. In South America, Australia, New Guinea, and Asia, they are called bird-eating spiders.

The salmon pink bird-eating spider is native to Brazil.

Sizes

    The largest spider in the world is a bird-eating spider. The goliath birdeater's body can be 3 inches (7.5 cm) long. Its leg span can reach 11 inches (28 cm). That is an impressive size!

    Most bird-eating spiders are not as big as the goliath. But none of them are small! The salmon pink bird-eating spider can have a leg span of 8 inches (20 cm). The barking spider's leg span reaches 6 inches (15 cm). The leg span of the New Guinea bird-eating spider is 5 inches (13 cm).

This goliath birdeater (below) is just a baby. Yet it is already much larger than a wolf spider or an Australian coin!

Shapes

Bird-eating spiders have thick, hairy bodies. Their two body sections are almost round in shape. The front body section is called the **cephalothorax**. It is protected by a plate called a carapace. The rear body section is called the **abdomen**.

The cephalothorax contains the spider's brain, **venom** glands, and stomach. Spiders have six pairs of **appendages** attached to the cephalothorax. There are two **pedipalps**. Between the pedipalps are two **chelicerae**. They are tipped with fangs.

Four pairs of legs also attach to the spider's cephalothorax. Claws at the end of each leg help the spider grip surfaces.

A slim waist connects the cephalothorax with the abdomen. It is called the pedicel. The spider's intestine, nerve cord, and blood vessels pass through it.

The **abdomen** is where the heart is located. It also holds the spider's **digestive** tract, respiratory and reproductive **organs**, and silk glands. The silk glands make the spider's silk. Spinnerets on the end of the abdomen spin the silk from the spider's body.

COLORS

Bird-eating spiders come in many different colors. For example, the goliath birdeater is completely brown. Species such as the Asian black bird-eating spider of Thailand are black.

Brazil's salmon pink bird-eating spider is mainly black, too. But, pink-colored hairs on the spider's body and legs make it look pink! Bolivia's steely blue leg bird-eating spider is also black. But, it has brilliant blue on its legs.

Barking spiders are different shades of brown, from gray brown to red brown. The purple bloom bird-eating spider from Colombia is a light chocolate brown. Purple patterns on its carapace look like a blooming flower.

The orange baboon spider has a starburst pattern on its carapace.

WHERE THEY LIVE

Spiders live on every continent except Antarctica. Bird-eating spiders are usually found in **habitats** with damp, moist air. Yet, some species have adapted to live in dry regions. Bird-eating spiders live in burrows, in trees, and on the ground. They do not live in spun webs.

Salmon pink, goliath, steely blue leg, and purple bloom bird-eating spiders live in South America. These spiders use their **chelicerae**, fangs, and **pedipalps** to dig underground burrows. Then, they line the burrows with silk.

Baboon spiders got their name because their feet look like baboon fingertips!

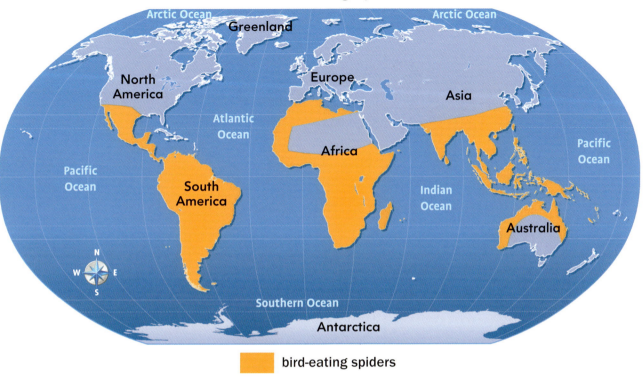

The Asian black bird-eating spider lives in Thailand's bamboo forests. It burrows into the undergrowth, where it makes a silken hideaway.

In Australia, the barking spider may live in dry areas or in rain forest regions. This spider digs a side burrow that slopes upward from the main tunnel. It can live there if the main tunnel floods.

Senses

Bird-eating spiders have eight eyes. But even with so many eyes, they cannot see very well. Most species are active at night, so their eyes simply detect light levels.

Because of their poor eyesight, bird-eating spiders rely on their other senses. They feel their way around their **habitats** using their hairs. The hairs on their legs and **pedipalps** are very sensitive to vibrations. They move when the air around them moves. In this way, the spiders can tell if there is a predator nearby!

The hairs are also helpful when bird-eating spiders are hunting. The spiders sense the movement of prey and then grab and kill it. Hairs help bird-eating spiders taste and smell their food, too. They do this through hollow hairs at the tips of their pedipalps and legs.

> To scare off predators, the goliath birdeater rubs hairs on its hind legs together. This makes a hissing noise that can be heard 10 feet (3 m) away!

DEFENSE

Bird-eating spiders have many enemies. Mammals, birds, reptiles, and **amphibians** like to eat them!

Some bird-eating spiders use camouflage to defend themselves against their foes. Even a brightly colored bird-eating spider is hard to see in its natural **habitat**. This causes some predators to overlook the spider.

In North and South America, bird-eating spiders defend themselves with special hairs. These are located on the top of the **abdomen** and are tipped with tiny **barbs**.

When threatened, the spider uses its legs to fling the hairs at its attacker. These urticating hairs are irritating to the predator's skin. If they get into the eyes or the nose, it can be very painful!

Pretend you are a hungry predator. Can you spot the bird-eating spider?

If these defensive measures do not work, the spider may rear back and threaten its enemy. The spider will also bite! A bird-eating spider's **venom** is not usually fatal to humans. But, its large fangs can deliver a painful bite.

Food

Bird-eating spiders are carnivores. And, they have big appetites! So, they are active hunters. They will eat any animal they can overpower.

Despite their name, bird-eating spiders usually do not eat birds. When they do, the birds are babies that have fallen from their nests. Insects, rodents, frogs, lizards, and snakes are more often on the spider's menu.

To hunt, a bird-eating spider leaves its nest. It hides in the underbrush and waits for prey to come close. Then, the spider grabs the prey with its **pedipalps** and bites it with its fangs.

The spider spits **digestive** juices onto its prey. The juices liquefy the victim. Then, the spider sucks up its liquid meal!

Bird-eating spiders got their name when an early explorer saw a big spider eating a bird. However, these spiders prefer prey that is easier to catch!

Babies

Bird-eating spiders mate once a year. Some bird-eating spiders can be aggressive. So, the male must let the female know he is not prey! Some species do this by quivering certain body parts. Others drum their legs in a special rhythm.

Male (left) and female (right) salmon pink bird-eating spiders mate facing each other.

This Chilean rose hair bird-eating spider (right) has just shed its exoskeleton (left). To molt, bird-eating spiders lay on their backs.

After mating, the female spins a silk pad. She lays between 100 and 1,000 eggs on it. Then she spins an egg sac to protect them. Depending on the species, the baby spiders hatch in 2 to 12 weeks. The baby spiders are called spiderlings.

After hatching, the spiderlings often stay near the mother. But soon, they will go their own way. Over time, the baby spiders outgrow their **exoskeletons**. They **shed** them in a process called molting. As adults, bird-eating spiders will still molt on occasion.

Bird-eating spiders are mature in about three years. Males do not live long after reaching maturity. However, females can live for about 25 years.

Glossary

abdomen - the rear body section of an arthropod, such as an insect or a spider.

amphibian - an animal that can live in water and on land. Frogs, toads, and salamanders are amphibians.

appendage - a smaller body part that extends from the main body of a plant or an animal.

barb - a sharp projection that extends backward and prevents easy removal.

cephalothorax (seh-fuh-luh-THAWR-aks) - the front body section of an arachnid that includes the head and the thorax.

chelicera (kih-LIH-suh-ruh) - either of the front, leglike organs of an arachnid that has a fang attached to it.

digestive - of or relating to the breakdown of food into simpler substances the body can absorb.

exoskeleton - the outer covering or structure that protects an animal, such as an insect.

habitat - a place where a living thing is naturally found.

organ - a part of an animal or a plant composed of several kinds of tissues. An organ performs a specific function. The heart, liver, gallbladder, and intestines are organs of an animal.

pedipalp (PEH-duh-palp) - either of the leglike organs of a spider that are used to sense motion and catch prey.

shed - to cast off hair, feathers, skin, or other coverings or parts by a natural process.

Theraphosidae (thehruh-FOHSUH-dee) - the scientific name for a family of very large, chiefly tropical spiders.

venom - a poison produced by some animals and insects. It usually enters a victim through a bite or a sting.

Web Sites

To learn more about bird-eating spiders, visit ABDO Publishing Company on the World Wide Web at **www.abdopublishing.com**. Web sites about bird-eating spiders are featured on our Book Links page. These links are routinely monitored and updated to provide the most current information available.

INDEX

A

abdomen 8, 9, 16
Africa 5
arthropods 4
Asia 5, 10, 13
Australia 5, 13

B

barbs 16
bites 17, 18

C

carapace 8, 10
cephalothorax 8
chelicerae 8, 12
claws 8
color 10, 16

D

defense 8, 16, 17, 21

E

ectothermic 4
egg sac 21
eggs 20, 21
exoskeleton 21
eyes 14

F

fangs 12, 17, 18
food 14, 18

H

habitat 12, 13, 14, 16, 18
hairs 8, 10, 14, 16
homes 12, 13, 18

L

legs 4, 6, 8, 10, 14, 16, 20
life span 21

N

North America 4, 16

P

pedicel 8
pedipalps 8, 12, 14, 18
predators 14, 16, 17

R

reproduction 9, 20

S

senses 14
shedding 21
silk 9, 12, 13, 21
size 4, 6, 8, 17
South America 5, 10, 12, 16
spiderlings 21
spinnerets 9

T

Theraphosidae (family) 4

V

venom 8, 17
vibrations 14